A Series of Colour

One Colour. Rouge

A novella by Sophie Constant

With thanks to all those who have supported me,

IBSN: 9781-291-27467-7

Chapter 1

Carmen Isabel Isolde gazed breathily over the cool morning scene, seated under an uncommonly lovely awning of an uncommonly lovely Parisian café. Beautifully dressed in a relaxed but tailored dress code she was a vision of off-white, fawn, and terracotta. She smoothed her skirt. A croissant and coffee was placed before her, and she smiled politely but took a moment before taking to it with a dainty knife. She raised her hand and smoothed a few stray hairs of her rouged brunette head behind her ears and looked up and saw the distal approaching figure, mountainous with false mystery lent to it by the overcast.

***

Dan was an attractive Aussie, a warm emotional man and retired athlete of 38 years. But you wouldn't know his age less he mentioned it which he rarely did. He was a big man, retaining still the muscular form of his previous life, through softer now he could still match most competitors in technique. He had been drifting. Searching for what he felt he had missed out on as an athlete. Sun-kissed hair had darkened with distance. He had been missing from his homeland for 5 years, less the odd romantic postcard to family back home. And of course letters to his mother on her birthday. He had a great smile. Offering him a lot of wiggle room in life though he didn't know it. He had bright softly melting blue to green eyes, conferring the sentiment of a clear ocean view.

He had started aged 33 in Thailand. With a bartender qualification in his back pocket he partied in Thailand. Tried Shrooms. Dropped Acid. Liked none of it. Met the girls of his dreams. Became a scuba diving instructor. He'd liked someone. He'd broken it off with Annan, or Ana or whoever or she'd broken it off, or rather there wasn't anything there in the first place but an old fashioned tradition in him had felt the need to say something.

He got a bus to Laos. Hated Laos. Loved the people. Got in trouble trying to be nice. Left some money and got a bus to Cambodia.

Loved the people. Still today, to mention the place, is to prompt a launch into nostalgia. The beauty of the people. Made a pilgrimage to the killing fields. Cried. It was cathartic. Volunteered at a school for a while. Met a girl. Left a girl. Went to Vietnam.

In Vietnam he bought a bike. And cycled to Ho Chi Minh City. It was busy in the city. He met a few Americans in his hostel, and they got drunk together. He ate sparrow. Was in two minds. Saw a B-52 submerged in a city water feature. Worked at a bar. Left the hostel. Met a fellow Australian on a bike who had a pregnant girlfriend in NZ, and on the spur of the moment they cycled to the train station and caught a train to Nha Trang. Met Veronica on the train. They exchanged email addresses but never kept in contact. He and his Australian stayed in Nha Trang for a bit. They met a scientist on leave for a week, she was swiss and worked at a conservation place. Dong something. Dong remaining in Dan's memory for obvious reasons. She was nice. She was intelligent, really intelligent but beautifully simple. He could never remember her name. Sandrine? Simone? Something hard to pronounce and French. She would make someone extraordinarily happy one day. He regretted not taking the trouble to learn her name. He visited a national park with her and the Australian who was thoroughly bored by all this.

She left. They met a bunch of guys from NZ, and got drunk. The accent made the Australian cry one night. Like a broken-hearted child. For hours. Dan held him.

They got a train to Da Nang, and Dan paid for the Australian's flight home. His name was Ted. He named his daughter Danielle. He got married to Janet. They had three more children, Ben, Josh, and Brodie. They moved to Melbourne. Dan would see Ted again but not for many years.

He was a little short of money in Da Nang. He met a German stranger, who was tall, fair and muscular. The German invited him to a bar near the airport. He explained that he was out here on business; in a clear but not completely clean English. Naivety led Dan to the German's hotel room. Having nowhere else to go led to the acceptance of a proposition. Desperation, and embarrassment. In the morning he heard the German leave. He rolled onto his back and looked up at the ceiling. His eyes watered slightly, and he covered his face with his hands. He took a deep breath, and moved his hands massaging his face. He rolled on his side and saw an envelope with his name on the bedside table. He frowned and picked it up. He opened it. Money. And a note with the German's name, number and address in Germany. He felt sick. And sore. But he needed the money. He showered and left

He found a church. It offered little salvation. He felt homophobic. Prejudice and cruelty were not natural to him. He gave his bike to a man genuflecting in prayer. He left Da Nang. He took a train to Hanoi.

He met a Vietnamese family, the Nguyens, three generations at a cycle hut. The elder of the family took a liking to him, and insisted that the family offer hospitality. Dan refused at first. But no was no option to this man. They had owned the cycle hut, selling, buying, refurbishing bikes and making helmets throughout the two older generations. The father Nguyen recently taking the helm of the business though the elder Nguyen still working but less so. Dan took to working in the hut. If business was good they insisted on giving him a small stipend but he was grateful mostly for the board they provided. The children had learnt English, and with some difficulty were able to translate between Dan and the adult Nguyens.

Dan liked living with this family, and settled comfortably with them. He became almost like a nanny to the children too. Their mother often leaving him to watch them when he wasn't working at the Bike hut. Father pleased by their getting extra practice in English conversation. The Eldest translated this sentiment for Dan. All the kids improved rapidly, but the Eldest became near fluent rapidly. Maybe because she was older, learned more advanced English at school, or just got more confident with the regular practice but Dan felt the gulf of language diminish daily.

The Eldest was a pretty young girl, of about 16. Dan felt mildly uncomfortable sometimes, she was always simply dressed, off duty in blouses of light colours or floral patterns and either jeans or a skirt. Sometimes she'd wear a simple summer dress. She was sweet. And had a lovely innocent smile. She had thick glossy hair, and wore two plastic hairclips, which matched her blouses. Dan always felt embarrassed seeing her in school uniform, an Ao dai, a long light blue smock shaped dress top over yellow pantaloons.

He liked speaking to her. And gradually she began to confide in him some of her worries finding freedom of speech in a language other's couldn't freely understand. She worried about growing up. Marrying. Would they take her far away? What would happen when Grandpa died? When Father got old? Who would look after the hut?

Dan did not know how to respond to these worries. But smiled in what he felt might be a comforting manner. She seemed pleased to have some one to listen to her anyhow.

He took her out once, with the middle and youngest. He often took the middle and youngest out. Swimming, maybe for a little treat, some street food and a walk. But she came along once after school. It was exam time and she'd been working especially hard on her studies. They had gone out to one of the bigger lakes dotted around the city. She had wanted to ask blessings upon her exam efforts, so they had gone to one of the temples. Dan entertained the two younger while she meditated on Buddha. He got them balloons. Afterwards they rented a boat and went out on the lake. The two younger were a little tired and peacefully laid back watching their balloons tethered to their wrists, lazily swooning in the sun. They began to doze.

Presently Dan stopped rowing, allowing the boat to drift lightly, not really going anywhere.

The Elder trailed her fingers delicately in the water, she looked up at Dan, for a while. She was formulating sentences in her mind. Presently she began to speak.

'Thank you. Dan,' she said unsmiling

'My Pleasure,' Dan smiled warmly at her

'Yes,' she said trying to fill space in the conversation.

'I hope the boat. Was not hard.' She said

'Not at all,' said Dan understanding her to mean she hoped the row wasn't difficult.

There was a pause again, as she looked down thoughtfully.

'I will sad, be sad. When you leave.'

It transpired that the elder Nguyen could sense something in Dan. He insisted on going away for a couple of days with the eldest child. Whether purposefully poorly translated or otherwise Dan wasn't sure where they were going. But they had bikes, and took a train.

The old man led them to the water, down a wooden path. And spoke to the eldest child while motioning out with the two fingers and one thumb of his right hand. Ha Long Bay stretched out before them.

The vision coupled with the kindness was the kiss of life to Dan.

They got a boat, and went to a bar set afloat. They drank beer, met some of the friends of the old Nguyen, veterans of the war. Laughed, played dominoes, loosely translated old war stories. Nepalm burns and blindness, B-52s and deaf in one ear. Boobie traps, rice fields and how the forests were never the same. They stayed with the elder Nguyen's sister in a small community afloat, where it was loosely translated that he'd left the community with a pregnant wife wanting more than to scrape by as a fisherman. Some sort of argument broke out which the child couldn't translate. Though Dan could tell by tone that old Nguyen's sister had never quite forgiven her brother for leaving. He felt a pang deep inside, and a small lump come to his throat. He wrote a letter to his mother though it would not be her birthday for a month or so.

The next morning all was forgotten, and there was a warm exchange between brother and sister. And a gift of fresh fish.

They ate it that evening with the rest of the family. Prepared beautifully by Mother Nguyen with rice. Not wanting to outstay his welcome, Dan made preparations to leave.

A few days later goodbyes, and bags packed he was walking to the station. He waited patiently in line. He heard a familiar Vietnamese accent with unusually fractured English. He turned and saw the youngest Nguyen squeaking and waving at him. His heart sank.

He followed her back home. Mother crying and being consoled by the eldest. Father was crying softly and staring resolutely at the bedroom door. The middle child watching him, tears streaming down his cheeks. Dan almost placed a hand on the shoulder of the youngest, but settled for the back instead. Old Nguyen was resting peacefully with a white handkerchief in his bed.

Dan agreed to stay for the funeral. He gifted a beautiful wreath. And though he was not loud in his mourning the family was satisfied by the sincerity of his tears. Father Nguyen threw a handful of the ground, and they waited a little way apart until Old Nguyen was respectfully covered. A fine dinner was shared later that day.

Dan bought an envelope and placed a little money inside. He drew a picture of Old Nguyen reclining on the boat, and a heartfelt letter of thanks. He wrote how much this stay had meant to him, though he knew it would be a few years until the children could translate. He felt that they would understand.

He promised to write them. He kept this promise, though it would be a while until his address was settled enough for them to write a letter of beautifully composed English back.

They saw him off at the train station a few days later. And later that evening opened the letter. They understood and cried as a family at the portrait. They saved the money, and read the letter a year later.

Chapter 2

He took a train to Beijing. It was time for him to be in Europe now. He didn't stay long in China, it wasn't the right time. He took a long train to Moscow.

His mother's birthday passed while he was in transit. He wrote her a letter.

He watched the countries change with wonderment, he loved that feeling. He marveled at the Gobi desert. He had his birthday the first night on the train. Some people he met had vodka with them, and bought a dessert, which passed as a birthday cake.

He met a beautiful Russian lady on the train, and engaged in an intense microcosmic relationship, which lasted the duration of the trip but for the last night. She admitted she was to be married. They never slept together. Dan always remembers the purity of that relationship with a small amount of pride. And mild disappointment. He is only human.

They both agreed that to attempt to keep contact was foolish and left it at that.

Frustration led Dan to have a primal one night stand with a Scottish lady, the same height as him. She was a handsome woman, an athlete herself. She was not ugly at all but not the type to appeal due to her presence. Dan had his reservations at first, but her bottle of Drambrouie changed his mind. And afterwards as his pleasured body drifted off involuntarily he was rather glad it had. When he awoke. She was fully dressed, sitting at the end of the bed.

He felt slightly awkward still naked and all. And cleared his throat slightly. He tentatively offered to keep in contact. She rebuffed this immediately, and sheepishly admitted that she was married. And that 'What goes on tour… stays on tour'. Dan was not happy about this. Not angry but he felt the need to add his tupenny 'Had I known, I would've said no,' The sincerity broke the tension, and they laughed. They added each other on facebook in a vague attempt to be friends.

He asked her to turn around, as he got dressed. He felt slightly insecure with his own body. It hadn't been long since it had approached physical perfection but a year away had caused him to relax. When he looked up, the Scottish lady was watching him. He froze. 'Um?' She laughed and said that she had to get a last look at a body like his before going back to her husband. Dan was somewhat mortified and secretly pleased.

He got off the platform in Moscow. It was cold here. And the air was different. Drier. Dan was used to the humidity of Asia by now. He fished an extra jumper from his luggage and was glad of the decision to wear trousers. He wondered a little lost on the platform.

The people who had celebrated his birthday with him spotted him on the platform. They smiled and waved and invited him to eat with them.

He had never eaten so much food in his life. Nor drank so much beer, or done quite so many shots, exceptional Eastern European shots. He entertained his hosts immensely. They seemed to love his accent. Somehow he managed to keep it all down.

He woke up unsure of how he'd gotten a futon or where he was. Kir was lying next to him awkwardly. He attempted to get up. A combination of the hangover of ages and the concern of disturbing Kir's sleep led Dan to abandon getting up for the moment.

He closed his eyes to absorb the quiet of the room, he could hear the gentle snores of Larisa, Nadya and Nina from the bed in the next room of the tiny apartment. Pavel was breathing heavily sound asleep from the sofa whereas Ilya had pushed two armchairs together. He was enjoying a surprisingly heavy sleep.

Dan opened his eyes. And started slightly to see Kir looking up at him. Kir had an elfin face, pointed chin but chiseled cheek bones. And cool blue eyes with closely cropped dark blonde hair. He was athletic, but slim, a diver. Kir moved into Dan. He grasped at Dan's t-shirt, and nestled his face to Dan's torso, ending shyly on his shoulder.

Dan was taken by the unexpected softness. Kir had been as loud as the others in tales of Russia, the benefits of communism, Marxism, singing folk songs early into the morning. He seemed delicate like this. And younger, closer to his true age. Shirtless, his skin porcelain pale in the cold morning light. Dan put a strong tanned arm around him, and held him close.

Pavel snorted loudly, waking Ilya. Kir pushed away. The moment was gone.

They woke the women to discuss what to do for breakfast. Pavel and Nadya had not been expecting to have anyone in their apartment the night they returned from their adventure in China. They were ashamed to have such little food in the house for the morning.

Dan grateful for their hospitality insisted on going to the supermarket for them. They were reticent to begin with but appreciated Dan's graciousness. Dan was happy with the walk in the cold air. He washed himself quickly, and drank a few glasses of water before trying to set off. Nina waylaid him, Kir was going too to split the costs. Besides. According to Nina, Dan needed to borrow Ilya's coat.

Dan was glad for the coat. He was tentative having Kir with him. After the tenderness from earlier. There was a sort of uneasy familiarity. Dan was still feeling slightly rough and Kir mistook his silence. He opened with good English in a heavy accent 'I, I am sorry for making you uncomfortable,'

Dan started. He wasn't traditionally uncomfortable. He considered his words quietly. He looked over at Kir and could sense his nervousness. He cleared his throat to buy more time.

'Not uncomfortable… just unexpected,'

Kir paused. Looking slightly relieved. More quiet.

They could feel the space between them diminishing.

'It's hard.' Kir inferred.

Dan let him carry on.

'It's not easy being…'

'Gay?'

'How do you mean?'

'You like men?'

'No. Yes. Maybe. Maybe not,'

Kir was blushing.

'I don't judge,' said Dan helpfully

Kir smiled wryly 'It's hard. I don't know. I can't ask. I can't try. I feel maybe I like men but then I get girl and I like this girl, we get on.'

'What happened?'

'She want marriage. She never say. But I know. She is 22. Of course she want marriage. She is educated. Smart. Beautiful. She gets job in government. All she needs now is a good marriage,'

Dan looks at Kir inquisitively 'So?'

'So,' Kir chuckles a little 'She leaves, engaged to Ilya! Marriage made in 6 months!'

Dan is visibly shocked 'Nina!?' Kir nods in confirmation, and laughs at Dan's reaction.

'I… I understand. I'm not happy at first. But I love Nina. Then I think to myself. I never could marry Nina. I knew she needed to but I knew it was wrong. I am… I can't explain-'

'You weren't in the right place?' Dan offered helpfully

'In place?' Kir frowned mildly with confusion

'I think I understand completely,' Dan nodded. Kir released a small smile.

'Then I meet men. But I see women. I don't know. I still have good friendship with Nina. It is enough. She is happy with Ilya. I think she will have baby soon,'

A longer pause. The supermarket looms.

'You did the right thing,' Dan looks ahead.

'Huh?'

'I was married once,'

Kir starts this time at this. Dan smiles.

'5 years, we met at 18.' Dan darkens slightly

'What happened?'

'She left me for someone who had more time for her.' Dan shrugged.

'More time?'

'I was a professional Judoka, I trained all hours, travelled a lot for tournaments, I did it for the love of it. I earned enough.' Dan looked at Kir 'I thought it was the right thing to do. Especially with everything she put up with. But in hindsight. I should've gotten more life experience –'

Kir sniggered

Dan grinned 'Not that kind of experience, just got out of the bubble I was in,'

Quiet emerged between them again as they entered the supermarket. They got their items quickly, eggs, milk,bread, bacon etc and reconvened at the checkout.

'You should go you know,' Kir began and trailed.

'Where?' Dan frowned wondering if Kir meant to go away '… go home?'

'To Judo. Pavel trains. He is very strong. I would too but Diving. I need to be ok.'

'It's been a while…'

Kir snorted 'Yes… but you never forget love!'

Chapter 3

Dan spent a couple of days in a freezing hostel, he met a couple of Scottish lads, two French students and some guys who he never really spoke to. He got to know the French men reasonably well in the few days of his stay. Fabrice, and Marcel were their names. They went out drinking a few times, and met up with the Russians from the train. There was a tense evening where Marcel got into a fight over who knew what. He was speaking a mixture of French, bad Russian and broken English to some putin supporter at a bar. Everyone else was engrossed in playing or learning Pacific ring of fire. A scuffle broke out, a bottle was broken. Fabrice pushed Marcel out of the swearing in French. Iilya stepped in as the guy swung this bottle around, catching Iilya's forearm. The man was swearing at Iilya who became immensely incensenced. Dan picked up the man on both shoulders with ease. He then dropped him on his back. And stood over the stunned man, pushing back Ilya who was trying to kick him in the ribs. Dan shook his head, and stared at this stunned man on the floor. The man caught his eye, and looked away. Dan helped him up, the man left.

Fabrice and Marcel were very grateful, they gave Dan their details, and invited him to stay with them during the semesters. Or, as Marcel had a family holiday home, Normandy over the summer months.

The French guys left shortly after. They went onto Poland.

Around this time, Kir invited Dan to stay with him and his diving team in their apartment. Dan was pleased to leave the hostel, it was lonely without the French guys, and cold to boot. Besides he liked Kir. He was a good guy, a nice chap.

It was a reasonable apartment, a little on the dark side but overall Dan found it comfortable and at least warmer. Kir introduced him to the other divers, his flat-mates Albert and Valentin. They were nice guys. Albert was really talkative, and Valentin was a quieter sort but all were brilliant hosts. Despite the sofa bed Dan took the floor in Kir's room, he was insistent though Kir tried to give him the bed. 'No, Kir, you're doing loads really,'

The divers had long training days, and Dan would be left to his own devices quite a bit. He spent time with Nina, Ilya, Pavel and Nadya. Spent quite a bit of time with Nadya as she was still a student and had odd times free. Russian coffees and cakes.

The one problem was that often when Dan left he'd have to wait for someone to be home. The diver's often didn't get in until pretty late. There was an evening where Kir found Dan waiting outside at gone 10pm.

'Dan? What are you doing man?'

'Waiting,' Dan was shivering, the cold of the night had set in, and he simply didn't own enough clothing. He had a bit of a boys night with Pavel and Ilya. The vodka swirling about his system was pulling Dan's body temperature down. He was groggy and confused.

Kir let him up, and guided him up the stairs. He put on the heating and sat him in the kitchen, next to the oven, which he then switched on and opened. The blast of warmth filled the small space. Kir opened the fridge –

'I've eaten,' Dan protested

'Ok, I make you drink. Warm you,'

Kir made Dan a hot chocolate with a big shot of Kahlua and a slug of vodka. It felt amazing to Dan. It possibly didn't help much with the grogginess. Kir turned off the oven but left the heating on. The other divers had gone out for the night. They all had the next day off.

Kir helped Dan out of his layers. He was shivering less now. Kir helped him into some trackie bottoms and a clean t-shirt and put him to bed. Dan was still too cold, though he didn't complain. Kir put on his pyjamas, and got in next to him. 'Turn around, I will keep you warm, then I will take the floor,'

Dan did as he was told. Kir hugged him close. 'Don't sleep yet,'

Gradually Dan's body calmed down. The colour returned to his face. 'I think, I'm ok now Kir,'

'You sure?'

'Yeah,'

Kir didn't move, he leant over and looked at Dan with concern. 'I get you. Extra blanket,'

Kir left. Dan nestled into the heavy bedding further. He reddened slightly, he felt unusually vulnerable. He could sense by the drop in Kir's English ability that he was really worried. Kir threw another blanket over him, tucking it around Dan forming a cocoon. 'I am worried to leave you,' he tried explaining. Dan had his back to Kir but could hear and feel something slightly plasticky being placed on the bed.

Kir got into his sleeping bag next to Dan. 'I sleep, for now. Just in case.'

Dan was strangely grateful to have Kir next to him. Though he knew he was mostly out of the woods it was oddly comforting to have Kir beside him. He fell asleep listening to Kir dozing lightly.

In the morning Dan woke up to the sound of Kir making coffee, he could here the whistling of the kettle on the stove. Dan rose a little shakily at first and pulled one of the blankets around him as a dressing gown. He walked into the small kitchen/dining room. Kir had just started to fry a couple of eggs and had put some batter into the house's waffle iron.

'Good morning,' he said with a smile.

'Morning,' replied Dan a little tenderly

'How are you feeling?'

'Better thanks,'

'Hungry?' Kir motioned as the breakfast feast he was preparing

Dan nodded 'I am somewhat,' he said shyly 'I'm sorry for worrying you yesterday mate,'

'No no I apologize – one of us should've been here,' Kir blushed with the guilt

'I'm ok though, I just need to eat and I'll be fine, maybe have a day in or something,'

'Yes, I will keep you company,' Kir motioned at Dan to sit, and wait while the eggs fried.

They ate. And Dan began to really appreciate Kir. He was kind of pretty, a small elfin hard angled face with a round forehead, a long slightly flattened nose, opalescent green eyes and ash blonde hair in a fussily cropped haircut. Short at the sides smoothly graduated into longer but still cropped front.

'You have a nice haircut,' said Dan making conversation,

'Thanks man,' said Kir unsure of how to take the compliment. 'My manager, my agent.' Kir struggled with the explanation 'My Diving, it's not forever,'

Dan nodded 'Yeah, makes sense, you're a good looking sort. I guess if you threw out your shoulder tomorrow wouldn't hurt to have another career,'

'Exactly,'

They had kind of a nice day. Peaceful. Kir folded out the sofa bed where Dan was normally installed. He got a couple of the spare blankets and pillows and popped them up on the sofa bed. Dan got comfortable, Kir brought out a jug of water and some biscuit type things and they settled to watch the entire Die Hard series in Russian.

Dan grew comfortable to the warmth of Kir, and found himself relaxing. He still felt rubbish, just generally unwell but he felt a pleasant wave of looseness work through his shoulders and back. As though he was unwinding. He dozed.

When he woke, he found Kir had dozed off too. He had wrapped himself around Dan in his sleep. Dan opened his eyes, it took him a moment to figure out why he was so warm. He wore a brief look of mild confusion but upon feeling Kir stir he quickly shut his eyes and lay still. He decided to go back to sleep.

Upon waking, Dan felt mild disappointment as Kir had moved. He was making dinner. Dan sat up, and shakily filled a glass of water, the jug clattered a little as he set it down. Kir hearing this came into the living room.

'You feeling better?' Kir sounded slightly shyer than usual

'Lots, thanks,' said Dan in between gulps.

'Good,' Kir shifted his weight 'I make food, stay I will bring,'

Chapter 4

They never slept together. Somehow it was never needed. But they had a good time. Quietly. Dan really liked Kir, he began to wonder about some of the things he thought he knew about himself.

They went to the zoo. During conversation a couple of breakfasts later Dan admitted that he'd never been to the zoo. Kir laughed at this 'Never!?'

'Never.'

'But man. It's the zoo!'

'I'm an Aussie! All the deadly wildlife is already on the loose!'

Kir laughed again, a deep rich laugh. Dan began to feel slightly defensive,

'It's ok,' said Kir wrinkling his nose teasingly. He reached over and placed a pacifying hand on Dan's arm 'Next day off, I'll take you,'

True to his word, they went. It was a clear cold day, and many of the animals from warmer climates were indoors. They looked at the insects, gorillas and white tigers. They laughed at the disgruntled camels, and were wowed by the dolphins

But Dan was really taken with the polar bears. He was taken by their grace and bulk. While watching one swim, he softly took Kir's hand momentarily. Kir dropped it.

They ate out afterwards. It was slightly cold on Dan's part. Awkward on Kir's part. The day darkened into evening as they finished dinner, and they made their way out into the dropping temperature. Dan began to feel cold. Kir moved closer into him and took his arm. Dan looked down, the soft brown spikes of Kir's fussy haircut were gently highlighted by the florescence of the night-time street. He sighed, his breath appearing in front of him.

Kir was beautiful, his soft warmth and his gentle weight. Dan felt a pang of disappointment in himself. He nuzzled Kir's hair, and closed his eyes momentarily with sorrow. In that moment however he wasn't ready for this time to end.

With time off the flatmates would often head out to see family or girlfriends. They might've suspected something, but if they did they were quiet. Dan and Kir would share more space during these times, they would sleep in the same bed. And they would talk.

They hailed in the New Year with a party with Pavel, Nina, and everyone else who'd Dan had met on the train. Incredible amounts of strong alcohol was drunk. Cake was shared. Dan awoke early hours later with Kir in his arms.

One day they went out to a market. Kir was inordinately excited about this particular market. 'It sells – how do you say – old things? Really Old things. And Not so old but um things.'

'Antiques?'

'Is that how you say it? Really old things?' Asked Kir brightly

'Like 100 years old?' Dan said almost lazily

'Yes. Maybe not that old. But old.'

'Yes. Antiques.' Dan paused 'Antiquities,'

'Antiques,' Kir let the word play slowly around his mouth 'Old,'

'-And collectable,' injected Dan bowing his head and looking at Kir in a scholarly manner

'And the other word?'

'I think it just collectively means very old things,'

'Ok,' Kir repeated the words a few times. Dan smiled at him sentimentally. Kir blushed slightly 'I'm sorry, it's good though. My English is much better since I met you,'

Dan pulled kir into his arms briefly 'I know,' he nuzzled his hair gently 'Your English is much better than my Russian,' he pulled away

They pulled on their coats and boots and headed out to the market. The mood was jovial between them. Friendly.

The market was pretty standard, just lined stalls, with tarpaulin awnings. Filled with all manner of antiques, lamps in one stall, old swiss army knives in another. Russians milling around going through the various stalls.

Dan had to admit he was bored, Kir was like a brightly curious child picking things up, going through this, that the other. Speaking Russian, throwing back comments in an excitedly deteriorative English. Dan smiled, and ambled behind not really paying attention. He let his mind wonder, the sky was a really clear blue, light clouds floated heavily across clear cold air. The cutting sunlight illuminated Kir's Blonde hair. He looked back and smiled excitedly as he picked something up. Dan reflexively smiled back, not really looking at him any more.

His eye fell on something about 10 or so metres away. He walked up to a stall which sold old cameras. He looked at them thoughtfully. He'd learnt photography when he was younger.

The cameras unleashed a surge of nostalgia, it ran deeply through him threatening to knock him off his feet. He thought of his mother, she'd been a photographer before him. After he was born too, but more domestic subjects, studio work. Before him she had taken assignments all over the world and had been hugely successful as he had understood it. So much so, that after him, they had lived pretty well on her savings, modest income, and father's salary as a carpenter.

She had taken lots of photographs of him growing up, dabbling in sport as he lived his Judo days. She said it was an interesting challenge. Like wildlife photography but indoors.

He thought back to them. His first medal, fighting spirit award. Him aged five in a tiny gi. His long hair phase. His shaved head phase.

He smiled to himself.

He picked up an old canonet, as it felt reassuringly familiar. And an EOS 888. Old and analogue now. But he remembered having wanted one in the 90s.

He cast a sidewards look, Kir was behind him.

"I'm happy you found something,' He said straight faced 'I was worried.'

'No. I was bored. But really thank you for bringing me here,' He looked back at Kir with an unusual dewy smile which Kir could not read.

He bought a variety of different Films, mostly Fujifilm. And a couple of batteries for the EOS 888. He couldn't stop smiling as he looked at it. It was rigged up with a lens for wildlife photographt. He liked the weight of it. The curves, the old smell, and the roughness of the rubber.

They began walking, Kir suggested something about a coffee, and Dan had nodded offhandedly. He looked up smiling still, and saw Kir, watching the street ahead. His eyes glazed slightly, as his attention was captured by a lady across the street.

She was stunning, in a lady's coat of camel coloured wool. Deep red hair and wearing a round furry hat. She clocked him with big green eyes, frowned then nodded at him.

He came to suddenly as though waking from the exciting part of a dream. He collected himself, and managed to nod back.

'You know her?' Asked Kir, looking straight at Dan

'Um no,'

And nothing more was said on the matter.

At the café Kir was slightly edgy with Dan, still as sweet as he'd ever been but there was an undeniable edge to him. Dan ran his fingers through his hair uncomfortably and tried to brush it off.

Chapter 5

Dan went with Kir to training a few days later. Kir's coach wasn't too happy but Kir was insistent. Dan smiled dumbly at their exchange.

Basically all Dan wanted to do was take some photographs of the divers training. Kir smiled at Dan reassuringly. 'It's ok, as long as they don't end up anywhere public, '

Dan nodded,

Kir turned back and was saying something to his coach in reassuring, submissive tones.

Kir turned, facing Dan his face relaxed into a anxious look. He nodded at him, his eyelids flickering as his motioned with his head towards the stands to the left. 'You can sit in the stands over there… no flash. And quiet.' He walked to the changing rooms under the glowering eye of his coach.

Dan wordlessly walked over and sat high up in the stands. He tried not to look at the coach. It was slightly awkward here. He wasn't sure what was between him and Kir if he was honest. He just knew his Dad back in Australia would not approve. And he knew that around others he had to keep a friendly distance from him. The flatmates were already teased quite brutally at times about Kir's new best friend. Dan frowned. He didn't know himself, but he was sure that Kir definitely loved women but would never be in love with a woman.

The divers came out. Apparently warmed up they stripped down. Dan half smiled gently to himself as he watched Kir in his natural environment. Kir in the scorching unforgiving florescence was apparently completely flawless. From a distance at least. He was laughing, clowning around with his team-mates. His hair was darkened in the harsh light. His body was beautifully sculpted by his sport.

He took out his camera and zoomed in, zoomed out. Focussed. He took two full rolls of film in the next couple of hours, one Fujifilm 1600 and a black and white roll. He was careful with the exposures trying his hardest to not waste a single shot. He let the last roll wind back the hum of the mechanics warming with satisfaction.

He left at the training break. Coming down to wave at Kir and offering to sort out some food for them later, casually. Kir looked mildly disappointed but relieved at the same time.

Dan shrugged it off as he turned and left the aquatic centre.

He had Judo in a couple of hours. The club he started going to had offered to pay him to train the younger judoka between 4-6pm. He checked his watch. 12pm. Lunch time. He stopped in a café to a solitary lunch and decided to finish with a strong coffee and people watch.

He checked his bank account on his phone, he frowned reticent to spend the money on getting the film rolls developed. He briefly thought about where he was going to go next. He frowned angrily at himself, and flinched catching his reflection in the glass of the window. He looked down into his coffee cup, eyes closing momentarily with mild shame thinking about Kir.

He looked up out of the window again clutching at the straws of reality. Where was he? What's going on? He was just losing himself in his thoughts when she shattered the glass over his mind. She looked through the window, at the menu, through the window again. He caught her eye, smiled in panic. Without looking at him properly her lips broke into a momentary flutter.

She came in, carrying a small suitcase and smiled a warm charismatic smile at the waitress, who charmed smiled back warmly. The waitress motioned to an empty table, she held up her hand gently smiling again and walked up to Dan's table.

'Hello,' BBC news English 'Do you mind terribly if I join you? I don't like eating alone,'

'Um,' stuttered Dan 'Sure,'

'Unless you've finished?' she said dropping her gaze to Dan's coffee,

'Oh no, I was going to sit here for a while anyway. I've a few hours to kill,' Dan felt that was a smooth save. He hoped so at least. She didn't leave.

She pulled out a chair, Dan was in mild shock and just a little too slow at getting it for her. She smiled appreciatively anyway. She took off her camel coat and slung her bag on the back of the chair.

Dan looked at her. He was at a loss with what to do. She watched him expectantly. Eventually placing her order. A healthy meal Dan thought appreciatively. She offhandedly ordered him another coffee, discreetly. Dan didn't realize.

'So…' She started 'What's your name?'

'Oh um.' Dan looked up at the ceiling having genuinely forgotten his name for a moment.

'Dan.'

Carmen watched him, her beautiful green eyes eyeing him again expectantly.

'I'm, Carmen,' she said almost helpfully.

'Sorry,' said Dan closing his eyes and shaking his head slightly. ''I'm a bit…'

'No, I'm sorry. I've obviously disrupted your thoughts or something,' her tone lowering uncertainly

'No. Not at all, I am genuinely glad for the company. I'm in a bit of a… thing at the moment and it's nice to have a stranger for company – if you get me,' Dan pursed his lips at himself 'I'm not sure if I'm making sense,'

'You are,' she said off-handedly 'I understand, sometimes it's nice to talk to someone you've just met. It feels kind of fresh. There's nothing pulling, nothing heavy,' She looked up her face clear, eyes as fresh as a stream

'Exactly, you can just you know. Chill.'

She nodded and was distracted by the appearance of her food.

The light coming through the window was clear but dull, it illuminated the porcelain tones in her caramel skin which with very little powder was nearly flawless. She began to eat neatly. She looked up, eyes momentarily squinting with social discomfort.

Dan cleared his throat. 'I'm sorry, I'm being really awkward.' He faced downwards, he looked up and smiled a disarmingly charming smile. He wrinkled his freckled nose and was on the verge at laughing at himself.

Carmen couldn't help but smile back. She had an unexpectedly pretty smile.

'So,' she said 'You're an Aussie?'

'Yeah, Melbourne.' He said reclining

'That's a good city,' she added. Dan nodded in agreement.

'Yourself?'

'British. London.' She said between mouthfuls

'All your life?'

'Yeah,' she said thoughtfully 'I still have a flat out in zone 5. West London.'

'Zones? Is that like…' Dan paused and sat up thinking 'Is that like districts or something?'

'Not really. They're travel zones. We have boroughs. But the travel zones kind of expand out 1 being central London… And 5…' she paused looked up and smiled wryly at some kind of in joke '5 basically being the shire,'

'The shire?' Dan looked out of the window momentarily 'Is that like-'

'Yeah. Lord of the rings. It's green and lovely,' She dreamed a little about home

'I'd like to go to London.' Dan sat back crossing his arms thoughtfully.

'Yeah? It's a great city,' she said 'The best,' she added quietly looking down pointedly. She looked up raising her eyebrows slightly at Dan who was watching her. 'Not that I'm completely biased or anything.'

They both chuckled.

'Are you living here?' She asked

'Sort of. Not really.' Dan looked deeply uncomfortable at this question

'Oh. Sensitive subject,' she raised her hands

'No no. Not really,' Dan shrugged averting his gaze briefly 'Really. I kind of ended up here. I meant to stay a short while. You know see the sights. Move on. St. Petersburg, maybe go to Poland,' He paused knowing the next question she would ask and trying to think of ways to answer.

'So what's keeping you here?' she asked neutrally

'Um…' Dan paused reddening, He looked up at the ceiling trying to conceal a slightly shamed frown. 'Um.'

'You don't have to answer. If it's an awkward question,' she said offhandedly

She finished eating and immediately called for the bill.

'I have to go I'm afraid,' She smiled 'Flight to catch,' She looked at him and nodded.

She got the full bill, for Dan's lunch too before he could protest. He started saying something but she waved him off. 'I've no time to quarrel the bill,' she said a little sharply. She stood up abruptly pulling on her coat. 'Sorry, I'm verging on late,' she smiled apologetically at him. Pulling at her suitcase.

She got to the door, and turned to him 'Email me.' She said

'Um. Ok.' Dan was taken by her momentum

'Carmen.Isolde@Rougegroup.com,'

'Sure-'

'You think you can remember that?'

'How do you spell Isolde?'

'As in Tristan.'

'Oh… That's really pretty,'

'Thanks.' She smiled at this

'Let me know when you make it to London. I'll make time,'

And with that she was gone.

Chapter 6

Dan left a tip. More really than he should've, but he felt strangely blown away by Carmen. He smiled at the waiting staff as he left. He opened the door and left taking a deep inbreathe with the sensation of the fresh cool. It had warmed up a bit since Dan had arrived in Moscow. He looked left then right but the vision of Carmen had dispparated, probably into a car.

He checked his watch. Time was getting on, so he walked briskly to the flat to pick up his judo kit in time for the 4pm Judo class. The slightly bigger kids, who would be either knackered out or hyperactive from the last lesson of the day at school.

He was slightly later than he would've liked, some of the kids had already arrived and were wondering about energetically in little Judo gis. Pavel already dressed nodded at him as he rushed in. 'I'm late,' Dan hurriedly admitted momentously continuing to the changing rooms to dive into his gi. The kids looked curiously at him as he dropped his bag. He looked around at their little staring faces and decided to get changed in the shower. He paused momentary as his put on his black belt. Knotting it. Thumbing the lengths as they fell neatly to his gi. He took a deep breath slight smile playing on his lips. Remembering briefly the day he got it.

Lineup. 8 fights. The first two were hell. Lasting with pauses beyond ten minutes each. A lifetime in contest. He was confounded. Barely managing the first, ippon (the win) by points. The second fight had lasted forever. He was run ragged by his competitor, managing to win only by a messy haggard effort of a half throw. He heard a distal yelling. His sensei. He was down a point in his third fight. Tired. But he had managed some kind of amazing comeback.

Twisting out. He had hit the mat face first. He remembered the smell of the mat and the distant burning of blood in the back of his nose. He had closed his eyes.

In the ashes of his tiredness, suffocating to the point of blindness he had risen up. Opening his eyes to see his competitor rising.

Before the referee could pause the contest on blood injury -

The competitor has stepped in for him. Sensing the finishing.

Dan had reacted. He had no memory of the exact moment, nor the point where his movement had evolved into a throw.

He just remembered the familiar sound of someone's back hitting the mat and the ippon puncturing the air.

He managed the rest of his fights after that moment. Having a drink with his sensei and the other candidate later that afternoon. He had shown up to the presentation ceremony a month later.

He smiled, as he walked out onto this mat. He liked the kids. He could hardly speak Russian, they could just about string some English together. With Pavel translating a little and the universal Japanese instructions they just about got a good class going. Dan was a great teacher; especially with the kids, he had a way of putting everyone at ease. They set up some fun warm up games. He spent most of the session assisting Pavel and allowing himself to be thrown for demonstration, and instructing on the couple of throws he knew well.

He stayed a few hours, instructing the older kids and then joining in the adult class in the early evening. At the end he smiled dumbly at his Russian classmates, had a quite polite chat with Pavel who invited him and Kir out on Friday.

Dan got changed, and waving politely left the dojo. He felt good for the exercise he could feel the vestiges of his old form returning. He'd never be as good, or maybe as he'd perceived himself to be good back when he was 20. Yet he was feeling at home again. A kind of calm confidence he'd not experienced before.

He got into the flat, and could smell Kir's cooking. He smiled internally. He had over the last week or so begun to feel a sense of unease. He hugged Kir from behind, Kir tensed momentarily before relaxing into his hold. He asked about the rest of Dan's day.

Dan dropped his gym bag in the corner, and leaned back onto the dining room table and talked about just going for lunch afterwards and then the Judo. How the kids were coming along, Pavel inviting them out.

Kir informed him that dinner wasn't far from ready, and Dan nodded. 'I'll shower for dinner,' he said walking to the bathroom.

As the warm water ran over him, he had a think. Carmen had made him think, what was her email again? He'd been in Moscow a good while now. It was just coming into the coldness of the Russian winter when he arrived, and now they were heading into the Russian Summer. In his mind he began to think of where to go next.

He finished up, put some fresh clothes on and came out to Kir just about plating up. The other two flat mates came in and busied themselves over their dinners.

'Oh thanks for serving me,' said Dan

'It's no issue,' replied Kir,

They both sat down to eat, and despite a lightly social din a slightly awkward silence coloured the air between them.

Dan cleared his throat. 'Kir. Do you want to go to Prague?'

'Oh?'

'I've never been,' Dan shrugged 'And I've been in Moscow for quite some time now.'

Kir smiled delicately almost to himself, He looked up at Dan, peering into his eyes, Dan felt a little self-conscious.

'Sure.'

Dan got ready for bed and as usual lay on the sofa bed. He listened out as everyone gradually turned in for the night. He got up and silently went into Kir's room. Kir still had on his bedside light, he was reading. He looked up expectantly and lay his book down on the floor beside the bed. Dan slid in under the covers with him, and Kir accepted him into his arms. Dan rubbed his nose against Kir's collarbone taking in the scent of his clean neck.

'You ok?' he asked

'I am,' said Kir

Kir asked Dan about his marriage.

'Why do you want to know?' Dan frowned, shifting uncomfortably.

'I'm just curious,' Kir shrugged 'I have not been married, what was it like? What was she like?'

'She was ok. I don't think we were well suited to begin with if I'm honest. I mean I loved her.'

'What was her name?'

'Lisa.' Dan smirked a little 'I thought she broke my heart. At the time, I was pretty broken up but I'm more philosophical now.' Dan wrapped his arms around Kir's waist 'Hindsight is 20/20 you know. She left me. And we weren't suited really. We got together for the wrong reasons, and when it came to it. We couldn't survive.'

'Oh,'

'I was looking for somewhere to belong,' Dan shrugged. Kir looked at him delicately.

'Are you still looking for somewhere to belong?' he asked in beautifully clear English.

Dan kissed Kir.

Kir was stunned for a second but melted into Dan. Wrapping his arms around his shoulders, Dan pulled Kir underneath him raising his hands to Kir's shoulder blades. He leaned in kissing Kir's ear and working down his neck. Kir pulled off Dan's t-shirt. Dan dipped away and into Kir allowing his t-shirt to come off in a smooth movement. He leaned into Kir again. Kir ran his hands through Dan's hair. He put his hands on Dan's chest pushing his body down deeper into Dan's flesh

His hands ventured downwards, Dan tried to ignore it. He kissed Kir again, pulling his body away. Kir was persistent. He pushed his hands into Dan. Dan's shoulders tensed. He tried to brush of the discomfort. Kir began gently stroking-

'Please stop,' Dan breathed

'What?' panted Kir

'I'm sorry,' Dan buried his face in Kir's shoulder before rolling off him.

Kir lay on his back staring at the ceiling.

'I'm really really sorry,'

'Please. Be quiet.' Kir's voice was hard, and quiet.

'It's not you, you're lovely-'

'I said. Be quiet.' Kir's voice was thick

Dan hunched up on his elbows, he hated what he was doing to Kir, with a morose sense of duty he looked into Kir's face.

Tears were welling up in his big blue eyes threatening to spill over.

'Kir,' he said gently

The tears spilled over glistening in the dim light of the bedside lamp. Kir said nothing and turned away.

Dan lay back, watching the ceiling for a moment, he got up to leave turning back to see Kir shaking slightly.

Dan felt a lump form in his throat. He wish he and Kir could work. He slid back under the covers. He held onto Kir, who tensed but unable to help himself relaxed into Dan's arms.

They said nothing more for the night but fell asleep like that.

Chapter 7

When Dan woke, Kir was already dressed. This was not unusual. But Kir was sitting on the edge of the bed, staring out of the window. It took Dan a moment to remember what had happened last night.

He sat up.

'When are you leaving?' Kir asked not looking back

'I can go this weekend,' said Dan with stuttered sadness mingled with shame.

'Ok,' Kir looked down at him knees. He turned to stand up.

'Wait.' Said Dan. Kir froze, Dan felt a cold fear in his stomach. Expecting the worse from Kir, Harsh words, more tears, yelling perhaps.

Instead Kir turned, leant in and kissed Dan on the forehead.

'You can stay here, on the sofa bed before you leave. When we meet Pavel on Friday that will be goodbye party,' Kir sat up still not quite able to look at Dan

Dan was relieved and slightly overcome

'Thank you Kir,' he swallowed the rising lump in his throat 'That's not what I was going to ask but, thank you,'

Kir sat eyebrows raised lightly

Dan looked at him, in his eyes earnestly 'I want you to know Kir, that I'm your friend, ok. My friendship is here if you still want it. I've been a shit. But if ever you're in my neck of the woods, my door's always open and my couch's always yours.' Dan paused, Kir's eyes softened 'I will heal.' He said shrugging 'I may,' he struggled to find his English 'One day.'

***

Friday night came along. Dan had packed he was planning to get the midnight train. They met at Pavel's and decided to all go out to a restaurant that doubled up as a bar with a club in the basement. Dan was quietly pleased with this. He hadn't had a proper out out in a while and things were still tense between him and Kir, getting wasted and going clubbing seemed like a great way to have a last hurrah in Moscow before moving on.

Dan checked his stuff into the cloak room and they ate dinner first up on the first floor, and had some pre-drinks. Everyone was there the girls Larisa, Nadya and Nina. The boys Pavel, Ilya, Kir and of course himself. Someone got the digital camera out for the cheesy dinner snaps, stalwart to everyone's facebook profile.

At dinner Dan noticed that Nina wasn't drinking, he looked at Kir who was deep in conversation with Pavel and his eyes flitted over with a knowing smile at Ilya. Ilya held his gaze seriously for a moment and then breaking into a guilty smile held a finger to his lips. Dan looked down to hide the onset of a sudden grin, looked up and nodded reassuringly at Ilya.

After dinner they hit the bar for a few more drinks. More photographs of them having fun. A few more pictures of them larking about with their favourite Australian. Larisa and Nadya planting a kiss on Dan's cheeks. The girls soon went home, hugging Dan in turn, lamenting over his leaving their group. He must write them, keep in contact, email. Dan was oddly touched. He smiled at Nina, asking her to let him know how she was doing every so often. Nina smiled graciously and nodded. They waved as they left noisily.

Then the boys headed for the nightclub downstairs. Loud music, flashing coloured lights and a few disco balls. Standard. Pavel and Ilya proceeded to get smashed even by Russian standards. Kir kept a little more sober as he had promised to see Dan off. They all had but Dan could already tell that Pavel and Ilya were going to bundle themselves into a taxi as this night for them had gotten messy.

Eventually out on the floor Pavel got dancing with some girl and disappeared for a bit. A drunken Illya came over to make incoherent conversation with Kir and Dan who had been awkwardly semi-talking at the bar under loud music. 'Nina is pregnant… but I haven't told you,' was the gist of his rambling. Kir congratulated him warmly and ordered a couple shots of vodka as a toast.

They looked around for Pavel, Dan touched Kir's arm, he flinched slightly. Dan awkwardly placed his arm by his side looking down. He looked up 'I'll find him,' he said. He took a couple steps away 'I'm leaving in a bit,' he shouted back laughing 'If I catch him fucking on the stairs at least he won't have to face me tomorrow!'

Kir chortled at this, Illya did not quite understand.

Pavel was found on the stairs, lipstick on his collar, neck, face, eyebrow. Yet was on his own. Dan suspected the angry reddening mark on his cheek was symptomatic of Pavel's lonely state. Dan laughed.

'She ditched then?'

Pavel replied in pissy Russian, which Dan could not understand. Dan sat down next to him. 'Girls.' Said Pavel 'At least. You don't have that problem.'

Dan gave Pavel a sidelong look. 'What do you mean?'

Pavel snorted 'I'm not stupid,' He leaned back 'I know you and Kir, had something going on or something,'

'Oh,' said Dan a little hollow

'Oh. Oh?' replied Pavel 'I am not so angry as others could be, it's ok,' Pavel shrugged. 'Me and Kir, we have know each other a long long time, since small.' He looked up at the ceiling as he continued 'I didn't think when we played as children, but we got older. And I knew he was different. Sure he had girlfriends. But I think. I know this man since we both fed as babies. Then there was this whole day, no not day. Whole, a –'

'His relationship with Nina?'

'Relationship?' Pavel paused sat up looking at Dan with drunken enquiry

'Like when two people get together,'

'Yes. They were together. Then Nina, she never ask. But she wanted marry. We all know. They were not together after. Then six months she marry Ilya. I talk to Kir. He was very very sad. Yes and no. He shrugged. He never said why they stopped. I know maybe and then on that train we meet you. And I see him. And I really know.'

Pavel stopped his head drooping forward, Dan thought he might pass out. He snorted and sat up abruptly again.

'You hurt him,' said Pavel, Dan wasn't sure if this was question or statement. Pavel shrugged 'He will not speak about it.' Pavel looked at Dan eerily 'He will not…' he searched for his English 'Say?'

'Admit,' stated Dan

'Yes,' agreed Pavel 'But it's good you go now,'

Dan looked down and smiled. He looked at Pavel still smiling. 'He's really lucky Pavel. To have a friend like you,' he gave Pavel a brief hug which was shaken off.

'Let's go toast Ilya,' Said Dan 'Have a drink. Illya's just admitted Nina's having a baby. But your not supposed to know.'

They went, and a drunken toast was had riotously. Dan shortly, pulled Kir aside and whispering in his ear 'I should head out soon,' he leant back meaningfully, his eyes sadder than intended. Kir shrugged, Dan smiled wistfully and with some sentiment Kir held his arm.

'Wait. I send these guys home before they embarrass themselves.'

Dan froze, looking at Kir dumbly. Kir raised his head, and stood straight.

'I will send you on your way.'

Kir went to put the others in a cold taxi, cajoling Pavel who still held the belief that he could drive in this state. Meanwhile Dan went to collect his things from the cloakroom. He checked his cash, having converted a large number of rubles to euros for beyond Prague.

He and Kir at agreed to go out front, and get the metro to Belorussky station. Kir should just about be able to drop Dan and make the last Metro home.

Dan came out into the cold, disorientated for a moment, he saw the figure of Kir, stride purposefully towards him, his hair lit up by the florescence. 'Come.' He said taking Dan's arm to lead him, then dropping it as Dan followed.

They walked in the cold night air to the metro, bought Dan a ticket, Kir already had a pass and sat under the fluorescing glare in the tin carriage. There was very little conversation, not through awkwardness now. Dan felt some kind of peace with Kir now but there was a kind of weariness, a gulf which ran between them. Dan looked at Kir's reflection in the window, and Kir flickered away.

Dan felt an end, but he was not sure if they would weather a start. He was grateful to Kir for doing this. And this is what he loved about Kir, he was just dutifully a good guy. Dan sat in Kir's space trying to hold on to a moment effervescing into a fine barely audible vapor.

All too soon, they were at Belorussky, and as it was late, Kir managed to get onto the platform to wait with Dan. The train was standing at the platform, but wasn't due for another 15 minutes, they walked to a spot where they could see out into the silhouetted darkness.

They stared out over the dark, standing under the white florescence of the platform. Kir looking resolutely out. Dan shuffled closer to him. He didn't think, daringly but gently he took Kir's hand. Kir thought about pulling away but he didn't. He sighed.

'Kir.' Dan looked, taking Kir's profile in 'Thank you.'

Kir smiled.

'For your hospitality. You've been amazing. I'm really grateful. And if you ever come to wherever I end up I hope to be as hospitable to you.' Dan looked earnestly at Kir.

Kir chuckled. He turned to Dan smiling. 'It's time,' he said simply. He looked a little sad for an instant but smiled again as he embraced Dan. Dan melted a little and hugged Kir back tightly 'Goodbye my friend,' said Kir

'Goodbye,'

Kir kissed Dan on the cheek and shook his hand as Dan boarded the train 'You have to leave now Kir, don't wait ok.' Dan worried glanced at the platform clock 'Don't wait, just go, and please let me know when you get in my Russian phone will still be in Russia for a few more hours.'

Kir smiled, narrowing his eyes playfully, the gesture gave Dan some hope 'Ok I will text,' he said taking a few steps backwards as he left.

Dan hung out of the carriage watching him go. Just as Kir was leaving, he turned one last time to wave and smile and then was gone.

Next in a Series Of Colours:

2 Colours, Blue

Please enjoy an extract of the next part of an exciting series of colours!

Dan walked through the shit-riddled pavements of Paris. A Canon 7D hung lazily on his hip. He was older, a little colder and a little stiffer these days. He was wearing a big Oceanic Teal jumper to stave off the November freshness. And light brown cords with brown boots. He was taking pictures for fun today, he was due in Kazakhstan over the weekend to cover the Grand Slam Judo tournament. He was looking forward to it, strange. It was strange for him to be behind the lens and back in Kazakhstan. But for the moment he was theoretically enjoying Paris. He could see her sitting down under an awning, at a cast iron table. He sighed softening at her loveliness. He photographed the moment.

***

Carmen wrapped a blue blanket over herself, and lay back in her seat. She left her laptop closed on the tiny white table and thanked god for business class. Keen as she was to sort through the million odd emails sitting in her inbox, instinct, her mind, body, even her soul dictated sleep.

She hoped to manage a couple of hours sleep before reaching Heathrow, power napping her way into a 1745 meeting at the office. Then she could crash at home in West London. Screw it. Take a cab. Pick up something from the deli. Then Sleep. For England.

Her neat little flat was just off the green in a particularly lovely but low-key part of West London. She was on the second floor, and had a wonderful view of the green, its line up of deciduous trees golden in Autumn and pinkish in Spring.

She got in. Kicked off her shoes and dropped her handbag by the coat rail installed by the door. She hung up her coat, and walked through to the kitchen throwing her Off-white Jacket on the sofa as she passed. She tried to ring Max, the worst boyfriend in the known universe. He didn't pick up, barely registering she put her phone on the sofa.

In the kitchen she got a plate, and plated up her dinner. A duck salad with quinoa. She popped in a fork. She got out a wine glass, and balanced it on the wide rim of the plate. She left the kitchen in a smooth movement, placing her iPhone in its speaker/charger and picking up its remote, switching on her evening playlist. 80s Motown at a gentle volume filled the flat. Followed instantaneously by a gentle two-step on her part as she picked up a half bottle of red from beside the speakers. Screw cap she grinned guiltily at herself. She stuck the bottle between her thighs and unscrewed the bottle. She put the cap back on the side and with calm, precision and the lightest touch she filled her wine glass still balanced on the rim of her plate.

She put the bottle on the side and picked up the wine glass. She headed for the window, and installed herself on the window seat. And got loose, melting against the wall as she relaxed completely. She people watched, she could see the bus stop opposite her flat, and had seen many mini dramas unfold there. She pulled off her skirt, and tights and ate dinner in her pants and work shirt. Because it was comfy and she can.

She was giving herself the afternoon off tomorrow. Besides she wanted to visit the shooting range. Alongside yoga, blowing open a clay pigeon was one of the more relaxing moments of her week.

And she needed to hit the gym.

She put her plate in the dishwasher, and polished off her wine. Taking off her shirt she went into her bathroom and put on her fleecy pajama bottoms and a fresh long sleeved tee. She brushed her teeth, meditated for 15 minutes, removed her make up and fell into bed, into a deep weary sleep.

She woke. Checked her phone. Conference call in 15 minutes, with just enough time to catch the 0751. Sorted.

She brushed her teeth. Had a good strong coffee. First of the day. Took the call. 'No. That is not acceptable and you knew my answer before you even came up with that.

I'm not being difficult. But we cannot reconcile our costs to that figure so I suggest you have the rethink.'

She politely finished the meeting and got ready to run for the train. Shower. Mirror. Eyebrow pluck touchup. Teeth. Primer. Liner. Mascara. Lips. Spritz.

To the bedroom. Picking out a pre-thought out outfit. Camel wrap skirt, Crème matt round collared blouse, burnt umber slash neck fine knit. Brown tights. Camel Jacket Camel heels in bag, flats on feet and she was away.

On the train by the skin of her teeth, she stood for the minutes to Richmond. Why a train for such a short journey? In the station she enjoyed her second coffee of the day and breakfast at her favourite in-station café. Some moments later, on the District line she awakened her Smartphone and began getting ahead on the early morning emails.

Delete.

Delete.

Rep- Delete.

Forward.

Reply

Delete.

Del-

Wait a second. She looked at the email address. DanielWilson@gmail.... She left it unread.

www.ingramcontent.com/pod-product-compliance
Ingram Content Group UK Ltd.
Pitfield, Milton Keynes, MK11 3LW, UK
UKHW020231250726
13967UKWH00001B/303

9 781291 274677